Llama Llama
Home with Mama
拉玛和妈妈在家

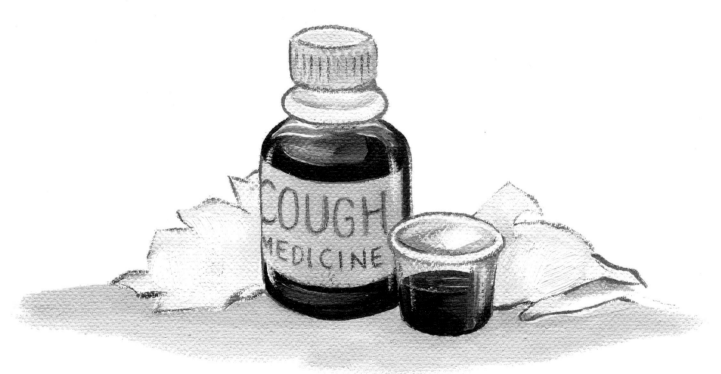

［美］安娜·杜德尼◎著绘　　雪　雁◎译

北方联合出版传媒（集团）股份有限公司
辽宁少年儿童出版社
沈 阳

Llama Llama, morning light.
Feeling yucky, just not right.

拉玛拉玛，天刚蒙蒙亮。感觉好难受，浑身不舒服。

Down to breakfast.
Tiny sneeze.

下楼吃早餐，打了个小喷嚏。

Sniffle, snuffle.
Tissues, please!
鼻涕流，吸一吸。
请把纸巾递给我。

Llama's head
is feeling hot.

拉玛的额头好烫手。

Llama's throat
is hurting **lots.**

拉玛的喉咙**好难受。**

Achy, fever, stuffy head . . .
Llama Llama, back to bed.

全身痛，发高烧，脑袋昏又胀……
拉玛拉玛，快快躺床上。

Time to rest.
No school today.

好好在家休息，今天不去学校。

Mama Llama
brings a tray.

妈妈端来一个装药的盘子。

Fruity medicine tastes **yucky!**
Llama Llama's throat feels gucky.

果味药，可真苦！拉玛拉玛，喉咙黏糊糊。

Look around. Not much to do.
Trucks are boring. Tractors, too.

四周瞧一瞧，玩什么才好？卡车拖拉机，全部很无聊。

Make a tunnel for a train?

要不，给火车修一条隧道？

Llama Llama, fuzzy brain.

拉玛拉玛，脑袋晕乎乎。

Mama Llama gets a book.
Have a listen.
Take a look.

妈妈拿来一本书，
听一听，读一读。

Heavy eyelids. Drippy nose.
Llama Llama starts to **doze.**

眼皮好沉重，鼻涕黏糊糊。
拉玛开始打**瞌睡**。

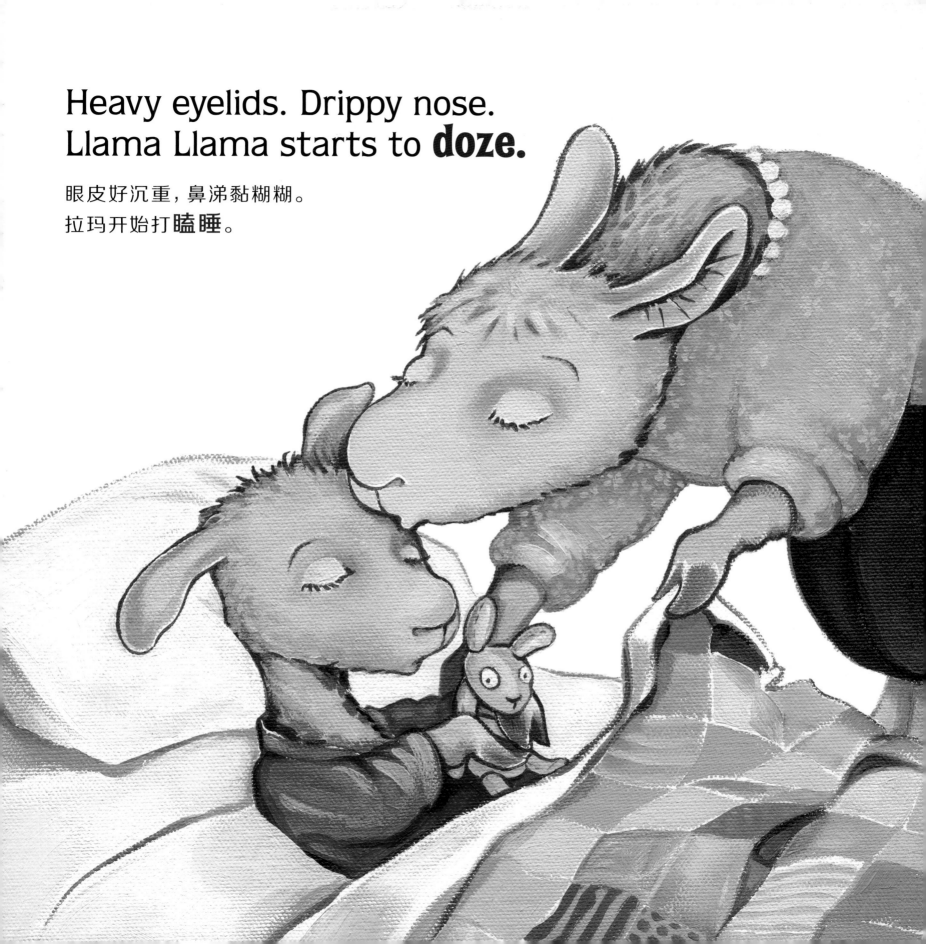

Up again and feeling better.

一觉醒过来，拉玛感觉好多了。

Draw some pictures.
Make some letters.
画一会儿画，写一会儿字。

Llama wants a sandwich, please!
Mama Llama starts to sneeze.
拉玛想吃三明治！妈妈却开始打喷嚏。

Lunch is over. Time for toys!
Mama's head does not like noise.
午饭吃完了，玩玩具时间到！可妈妈头很疼，不想被打扰。

Mama makes a
big **ah-choo!**

妈妈打了个大大的"阿——嚏"!

Llama's out
of things to do.

拉玛什么也做不了。

Uh oh! Mama's
throat is sore.

哎呀！妈妈的喉咙痛。

Being sick
is such a **bore.**

生病的感觉真糟糕。

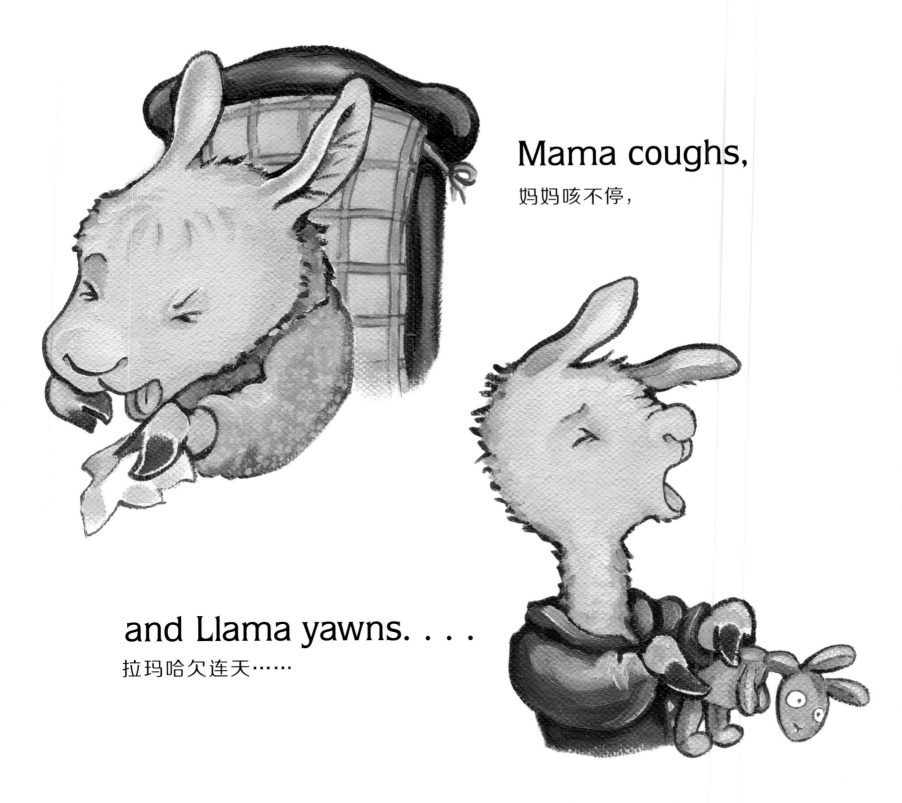

Mama coughs,

妈妈咳不停，

and Llama yawns. . . .

拉玛哈欠连天……

How long can this day go on?

今天可真是漫长呀。

Mama shnortles, hacks, and wheezes.

妈妈抽纸巾，擦鼻涕，直喘气。

Llama Llama's **sick** of sneezes!

拉玛拉玛，讨厌打喷嚏！

湿湿的纸巾，一团团，黏糊糊。

Soggy tissues,
gobs of guck.

Sniffing,

抽鼻子，

snorting,

吸一吸，

Llama Llama, red pajama,
sick and bored, at home with Mama.

拉玛拉玛，穿着红睡衣，和妈妈待在家，难受又心急。

WAIT! Llama Llama knows what's best.

等等! 拉玛拉玛, 有了好主意!

Mama Llama
needs a **rest!**

妈妈需要休息！

Get more tissues.

拿一盒卫生纸，

Bring a cup.

端来一杯水。

Fluff a comfy pillow up.

把舒服的枕头抖松软。

What else could Mama Llama need?

妈妈还需要什么呢？

How about some **books** to read?

看看书怎么样？

Just the thing for Llama Llama,
sick at home . . .

就像妈妈照顾拉玛一样，当妈妈生病待在家……

拉玛也会陪伴她。
but with his mama.

献给喜欢跟妈妈待在家里的

莱德利和雷顿。

图书在版编目（CIP）数据

拉玛和妈妈在家：汉英对照 / (美) 安娜·杜德尼
著绘；雪雁译. — 沈阳：辽宁少年儿童出版社，2019.1
(2019.4重印)
（羊驼拉玛系列）
书名原文: LLAMA LLAMA HOME WITH MAMA
ISBN 978-7-5315-7424-8

Ⅰ.①拉… Ⅱ.①安… ②雪… Ⅲ.①儿童故事—图
画故事—美国—现代 Ⅳ.①I712.85

中国版本图书馆CIP数据核字(2017)第273009号

LLAMA LLAMA HOME WITH MAMA
Copyright © Anna Dewdney, 2011
This edition published by Viking ,
Penguin Young Readers Group
Simplified Chinese edition copyright:
2017 Beijing Baby-Cube Children Brand Management Co.,Ltd.
All rights reserved.

著作权合同登记号：06-2017-263